CANTEND

CANTEND

AND SO IT BEGINS

VIDHU KOTA

PARTRIDGE
A Penguin Random House Company

To order additional copies of this book, contact
Partridge India
000 800 10062 62
orders.india@partridgepublishing.com

www.partridgepublishing.com/india

CONTENTS

Acknowledgement

I would like to thank my family **FOR THEIR INSPIRATION FOR ME** to write.

All the facts in the book are not true. For example, the count of people in the years mentioned in the book cannot be possibly true.

I would further like to thank Rick Riordan who inspired me and brought me to the world of writing.

I am indebted to Dilip Bhayya for his time and efforts in bringing out the characters in the book alive through his illustrations.

PROLOGUE

Year 5025

Scientists will discover that in thirty-nine years, the land of the world will be destroyed. Keep in mind, not the atmosphere. So the best of architects, scientists, scholars, and teachers came together to make 'The Flat Earth[1]', a flat replica of the earth, 100,000,000,000,000,000 feet above mean sea level. They somehow made arrangements for oxygen, water, food, cultivation, and all the basic necessities we need to live. And it had all countries, states, oceans, and even villages exactly copied, and it had enough space for 200 billion people or simply for the whole population of 100 billion plus by the end of the millennium.

---

[1]   The Flat Earth is not oval in shape and is just flat.

Year 5063

A year before the end of the Earth, every living organism was transported to 'the flat earth'. The Earth was destroyed in 5064, and the people started thinking that the destroyed Earth had no piece of land left.

But some believed that the re-created Grand Canyon on flat Earth had no end and this was the only way to reach the destroyed Earth, if anything left. They started calling this entrance of recreated Grand Canyon as 'Cantend'.

Year 5076

Famous Scientist Norm K. went to explore Cantend, but he never came back. Thus, the story begins.

***

THE KENZYS

Year 5079

Five years old Dane Kenzy was looking out of the window, when his mother, Elsa, shouted, 'Dane, it's story time!'

Dane looked back. 'Coming, Mom!'

Dane got into his baby car and started the engine.

Dane was a normal boy with black hair and brown eyes.

He was wearing black, his favorite color, and navy blue jeans.

Dane finally reached his room.

Elsa was in Dane's room reading a book on the Ipad 7965443568 mini air.

Yes, an Ipad 7965443568 mini air!

When she saw Dane, she closed it and put it on the table. Dane got on to the floating bed.

'What story does Dane the Great want to hear today?' Elsa asked.

She used to work at the Icy Amusement Park. She had blue eyes and blonde hair. She was still wearing the uniform of the Icy Amusement Park.

Dane got many passes every month and also many souvenirs of the Icy Amusement Park—for free!

'MANDRELA!' Dane replied.

'Okay Let's begin. Long ago, around 3086, there—'

Dane interrupted her,

'When is Papa coming?'

Every night, Elsa heard the same question, 'Where is Papa?'

And she answered the same thing.

'You know, Papa has gone all the way from Arizona to Paris. He'll come eventually.'

Dane then whispered, 'How can it take him three years? Okay, no story today. I'm sleepy.'

His father was Norm Kenzy.

***

THE TRUTH

Year 5084

Dane was now 10.

He was in the ground floor of his house on his dining table eating rainbow choco cubes.

He now looked smart and with a ton of attitude.

His confidence reaching the sky, and he was so fit that he looked like he ran across the world and then never ate anything except carrot juice and tomatoes.

He was wearing, of course, a black shirt and blue jeans.

He picked up the Times newspaper and read it aloud.

'Apple releases Ipad 20000000000000'

'Gramak Obama becomes the President'

'Only 300 people living on Mars are transported to Neptune for death ceremony of President of Neptune, PittySoocker Pants.'

'Blah, blah, blah, the same daily news. Idea!' He suddenly yelled.

'What's the matter?' Elsa asked while washing the dishes nearby in the wide washbasin.

He didn't answer; he just wore the voice headphones and said, 'Computer, show me the Times issue of . . . uh . . . 5076, maybe.'

Suddenly, a screen appeared before him.

His eyes burst out when he read the headlines. It clearly said, 'Greatest scientist of the era Norm Kenzy goes to explore Cantend and doesn't come back'.

'Mom, why didn't you tell me this before?' Dane said without any expression on his face.

'What son?' Elsa asked.

'About dad and Cantend. You lied for five years that he is in Paris. I always wondered how he could be in Paris for eight years, but I never asked.'

Dane said with the same blank expression on his face.

Suddenly, Elsa stopped washing the dishes, and she ran to Dane and hugged him. 'I'm sorry son that I didn't tell you. I thought that telling you about it would spoil your future life and career. Tell me if there is any way I can make up.'

Then they remained in silence for a long, long time with tears in their eyes.

***

THE PROMISE

Suddenly, Dane said, 'Actually, you can make up! But promise me that you'll swear on Dad that you will not say "no".'

Elsa thought for a while *he is only 10, what can he ask for?*

And then said, 'Okay! I swear on Dad that I'll not say, "no".' She wiped her tears.

Then Dane took a long breath, wiped his tears too, and said, 'When I'm 13 and eligible to drive a several-multi-wheeler, you'll get three of them. I'll make some friends and go to explore Cantend.'

'But,' Elsa started to say but was interrupted by Dane.

'You promised!' Dane whined.

'NO! I can't lose my son!' Elsa said.

'Mom, you will not lose anybody. Dad will also be proud, and I promise nothing will happen to me!'

Dane said, staring directly into his mother's eyes.

'No, I cannot allow you Dane. I am really sorry. It is too dangerous!'

'NOTHING WILL HAPPEN TO ME, MOM!'

'Okay, I allow you, but promise me you'll be safe.'

'Mom, chill! There are like three years left!'

***

F<small>RIENDS</small>

The next day.

In school, Dane was wondering that whether using plastic as fuel is possible or not when Mrs. Witched, or The Witch as Dane called her, yelled.

'Students! There are new students today! Susan Law and Trench Carl.'.'

Dane thought that her voice was no less loud than a one-ton TNT bomb.

Dane Kenzy

Susan Law

Trench Carl

Then she said, 'Introduce yourselves, and be seated!'

Two people entered the room. A thin girl with red hair and blue eyes, wearing a red bright shirt and blue jeans followed by a fat boy with black hair and green eyes, wearing a XXL sized grey t-shirt with a chameleon on it and plain black trousers.

The boy said, 'My name is T...Trench Carl... aged 10. I'm from New... Jer ... Jersey, and I like exploring...' Then he let out a big sigh and sat in front of Dane.

Then the girl came forward. 'My Na ... name is Susa . . . Susan Law. I'm 10, and I'm . . . from . . .

New . . . Jer . . . Jersey. Also . . . I like advent . . . Adventures,' she said and sat behind Dane.

Dane noticed they both were sweating when they spoke.

So, he said without turning his head either ways. 'You're hiding something, right?'

They both were shocked and turned their head towards Dane.

'N . . . no! I don't even know that person,' Susan said.

'Susan, we need to tell him. It was our oath . . . remember?' Trench said almost whispering.

'Okay, but in the recess, we are new in school and need to catch up. This is midterm,' Susan said trying to relax herself. Trench nodded.

'Now, students . . . take out your mechanics textbook!' The witch yelled.

Recess of a back story.

TRINNNGGGGGGGGG! No, reader, it's not your doorbell. You do not need to get up to open the door. The bell rang at Dane's school, and Dane, Susan, and Trench ran outside really fast and went to one corner of the school garden.

'I'll begin,' Trench said, 'My parents are Mark Carl and Hannah Carl. And Susan's parents are Flint Law and Pepper Law. They—'

'Aren't they the top two billionaires of the world?' Dane interrupted.

'Yes,' Susan replied ignorantly, 'They both wanted to be better from each other and also different from each other. My parents abandoned me as they wanted to save the expenses they would have to spend on me, but unfortunately, Trench's parents thought of the exact same thing.'

Then, Trench said, 'They left us in garbage cans until Aunt Margr—'

'Stop!' Susan suddenly shouted. 'Our oath was only to tell the reason behind our decision. Okay, Dane, the main reason is we are damn unlucky, and this unluckiness isn't any better than to die! So yeah, we are going to die as soon as possible.'

Dane's mouth was wide-open and eyes dull. He said, 'You cannot stop in between—not a cliff hanger! Okay, it's your oath.'

Dane said sighing out loudly. Suddenly, he got an idea and said, 'Okay, guys, I got a really good idea! Listen, my father is Norm Kenzy.'

'Isn't that the scientist who went to explore Cantend and never came back?' Trench yelled.

'Yes… When I'm 13 and eligible to drive a several-multi-wheeler, my mother is getting three of those, and I am going to explore Cantend, and I'm likely to die, so . . . will you guys . . . mmm . . . will you join me?'

Trench and Susan looked at each other and said, 'Only if you don't forget this.'

Dane nodded. 'No, I'll not forget.'

Then, they put their hand on top of another and Dane said, 'To find my dad! Maybe!'

Then, Susan and Trench nodded and yelled. 'To die!'

The trio had been formed.

***

SKIPPING TO 5087—THE DAY

'Happy birthday!'

Dane heard a grim voice as he woke up. It was 9 September 5087. It was the day of hope, a day of discovery, a day of risk, a day of . . . I don't know . . . finding-dancing penguins, maybe. Anyway, let's get back to the story.

Yeah, so it was Elsa wishing him. 'Good morning, mom!' Dane said trying to sound cheerful.

Elsa smiled sarcastically, and handed him a duffel bag. 'These are all the necessities needed for your travel food, extra clothes,' Elsa said hurriedly.

'But, Dane, you sure you want to do this?'

Dane gave her a smile. 'Yes, mom. Dad would have done the same for me. I'll be safe. I promise.'

'I know you'll be safe, but what if something—' Elsa started to say but was interrupted by Dane.

'There is no "if", mom. I'll be safe, and I know it.' Elsa sighed

'Okay, now get ready. Your friends are waiting outside.'

Trench and Susan were leaning on the Triple-Multi-Wheeler (TMW) that Elsa had bought instead of buying three different several-multi-wheelers.

Trench and Susan were wearing the same clothing they wore when they met—although a bigger size.

Trench suddenly asked, 'Do you think this will work?' Susan looked at him straight in the eye. He was used to that.

'What do you mean?'

Trench thought for a bit and said, 'I mean, you sure we'll die. I mean our unluckiness can spoil it. You remember the time when we jumped off the 78th floor of the orphanage?'

'Yeah, we landed on a truck carrying pillows. But, dude, this is Cantend. No one ever came back!' Trench nodded, and Dane came out running from his house

'(Huffs and puffs) Ready to go guys!' He was carrying luggage that probably weighed more than Trench, and that, sir, is a lot.

Trench and Susan looked at each other as if they were saying 'Why?' to each other. Dane opened the back, put the luggage, and stretched his muscles.

'Today is a big day guys,' Dane said as Elsa came out with a flood of tears.

Dane saw her and ran to her. 'Mom!' He hugged her.

Then even Susan and Trench were crying, and Elsa signaled them to hug her too.

'Be safe.'

Then they got in the TMW and drove off to Grand Canyon. Dane, in the TMW, said meekly,

'Bye, mom.'

***

THE FALL

It was five in the morning when they reached the entrance of Cantend—the Grand Canyon.

People were were flying to their jobs on their hover shoes. There were skyscrapers everywhere. No one really seemed to notice that there was a TMW right at the edge of the Grand Canyon, and because there were no robberies or anything that happened in this year, (oh, and also no one tried to jump off the Grand Canyon) there were no security guards appointed. And then, they jumped. Or actually, they fell.

Now seven hours had passed since they fell.

'Susan, I wonder why I never asked this, but if we keep falling, how the hell will we die!' Trench yelled.

'I didn't think of that either. Dane, how're we going to die!' Susan yelled. 'Dane?'

Yes ladies, gentlemen, boys, and girls, Dane Kenzy the great had fallen asleep at the most critical moment of their short life.

'Dane!' Trench said slapping him.

'Who! What! Where!' He suddenly yelled.

'How will we die?' Susan asked politely.

'I don't know. People say that if there is a low pressure when you fall, your blood vessels burst, and you die.'

Trench banged his head on the control system. 'Dude, one we are flying, and two this is a pressurized cabin!'

Suddenly, the computer said,

'System error, engines failing.'

'Yay, our luck's working!' Susan said shaking Trench's shoulder. His cheeks were moving uncontrollably.

No no no no no no! Dane said to himself in a low voice.

The TMW was heating up like a gold ring put in ten thousand degrees Celsius hot water.

'AHHHHH! I didn't know that dying involved so much pain!' Susan yelled.

The TMW was now traveling at a speed of light.

BOOOOOOOOOOOOOOOM! Everybody fainted.

***

<u>OH MY GOD</u>

'We've landed!' Trench said shaking Dane's shoulder as if pigs were flying or elephants were doing gangnam style.

'What are you saying? Oh my goodness!'

Dane said opening his eyes.

'Oh my god!' Trench yelled.

'Oh my god!' Dane yelled.

'Oh my god!' Trench yelled.

'Oh my god!' Dane yelled.

This kept going on for like three minutes, and then Susan slowly woke up.

'What is the matter you guys? Oh my god! Oh my god! Oh my god! Oh my god! We've reached the end of Cantend!'

Trench whined. 'What is up with our luck?'

Dane was still shocked. 'Guys, should we get out?'

'Yeah, maybe, we'll die without oxygen,' Susan said with a little hope.

The trio then came out.

Then there were millions of beings, blue humanoids with large eyes, stared at them like they were—actually, I can't say that they were other beings, but yeah, they were staring at them.

They were in a large place, a sort of kingdom with high-end large castles and small houses. There were millions and millions statues of seahorses and cockroaches. There were also many ponds with lava and also some with water! Many things were made up of gold and other blue stuff. In front of them was the largest castle. It looked majestic and awesome. It had a futuristic design, which held it apart from rest of the kingdom. It glowed in blue neon with black tiles.

And then all of the beings bowed.

'Oh my god,' the trio said.

***

Vidhuslovia

'All hail to the new rulers!' A being yelled. Then the other beings yelled together. 'All hail!'

'They need time to get rid of the shock—DISPERSE!'

Then, all the beings disappeared. The being was maybe the minister or something. He wore a weird red scarf around neck with a golden border. He kept his two fingers on his temples and said

'Hello rulers Dane Kenzy, Susan Law, and Trench Carl. I'm going to teleport you to your separate tents to explain you stuff and equip you.'

And then blackout And then Dane was in a tent with the minister.

'Hello, Prince Dane. I'm Ryanpathaksaintali. Errr . . . you can call me Ryan.'

Then Dane slowly opened his mouth, 'Uhhh . . . Ryan, what is this place?'

Ryan sighed. 'You, sir, are in Vidhuslovia, which you might call Cantend. This place is a young and developing place and was made around twenty-three years ago.

A scientist, who came from above, made it. He came, like you, in a ship. He was doing an experiment in which the first two Silleroids were made. That's our species by the way called Woolaf and Falsewagen.

They were much bigger and much more powerful than us. Then he made many more Silleroids who looked like us, and then, the scientist became king of Vidhuslovia. But then, Woolaf and Falsewagen thought they were more powerful to be king. They ejected all of the king's chemicals into them. Then they became insane, large, powerful, mad beasts. They kidnapped the King and put him in a jail they made far away. From that day, Vidhuslovia had no ruler, and we made a rule that whoever came from above, would become the ruler.' Dane thought for a bit .

'Wait, what's the name of the scientist?'

'Norm . . . why?'

'He's my father... I need to get him back.'

'I predicted this. You and your friends need to take your weapons created by the best forgers. Choose between this wide range.' Ryan said clapping his hands.

A board appeared with a lot of weapons. He first took a sword.

'What's this?' he asked.

'Ooooh . . . my personal favorite, the Absorn sword. It absorbs any solid material its tip touches.' Ryan said.

Dane kept it aside. Next, he took some kind of boots. 'The Runon boots, wearing this, you can run at a speed of 950000 km per hour, and you can run on anything.'

Dane looked fascinated and kept it aside too. Then he took a bracelet.

'Touchyinvis band, it makes you invisible and untouchable whenever you want.'

Dane kept it aside too.

'Okay, so be ready and come outside.' Ryan said and went outside.

TRAINING

Dane went out to meet his friends. Trench had a trident with him

He was wearing some gloves

And was on a hover board.

And Susan had a bow with an aimer.

She had ring and some weird shoes.

'Hey!' Dane yelled and told them about his weapons.

Then Susan said,

'This bow shoots arrows that follows the one it was aimed at. This ring creates a force field which deflects the attack, and with these shoes I can jump really high.'

Then Trench said, 'This trident can create natural disasters which will only hit the target. This creates an unbreakable temporary wall, and this is a foldable hover board.'

Then Susan said, 'Guys, I know these weapons are really awesome and every thing, but the bad thing is we really need to avoid being killed here.'

Trench sighed and nodded and Dane asked,

'Why is that so?'

'Oh, so that perso . . . sille . . . whatever didn't tell you, huh? If we die here, our spirits will keep roaming in this world. And so, when we stepped on this ground, we became immortal. That means we can live forever. Old age or diseases cannot kill us, but if one attacks us and damages us seriously, we can die,' Susan said. Then suddenly, Ryan appeared from nowhere.

'So, are you, highnesses, comfortable?' Dane suddenly remembered and said,

'Yes, we are. Now tell me where is the layer of Woolaf and Falsewagen!'

Dane suddenly started running towards a random point.

Then Ryan quickly held his hands, but Dane didn't stop.

'Stop your highness, you are not yet ready!' But Dane didn't stop.

"You've left me no choice your highness, thungrase!' Ryan yelled.

Dane got an electric shock, and he knelt down. 'What the hell just happened?' Dane asked, surprised.

'I'm sorry your highness, but you were not stopping,' Ryan said being sorry.

'It's okay, but what did you do?' Dane asked curiously.

'Oh, nothing, I just used a magic spell. You are going to learn them too in your training.'

Ryan said.

'Training?' Trench asked.

'Yes, you didn't think that you can face Woolaf and Falsewagen without any training, did you?' Ryan said, 'Your training will start tomorrow dawn. For now, you'll be teleported to your castle chambers, and here are your timetables.'

Ryan handed them sheets of paper. 'All it says is training,' Susan said.

'Exactly!' Ryan said disappearing, and even the trio disappeared.

Dane was now in his chamber, dressed in awesome royal clothes. The bed was made of pure gold, velvet, silver, and bronze and every other beautiful material. The room had a pleasant aroma, which reminded him of his mothers hair. Dane was too tired and confused to admire the beauty. He slept in a blink of an eye.

***

DAY ONE

At dawn, when Dane was still sleeping, *WHOOSH!* And then *THUD!* Dane was teleported to a field and fell on the ground. He suddenly woke up. He was in a tracksuit. 'What happened?' Dane yelled.

'Your highness, you weren't waking up with the mind alarm, so I had to teleport you,' Ryan said with three more people . . . no, Silleroids. Surprisingly, even Trench had woken up and was there!

'Okay, let's start training. Go to your stations,' Ryan said. Dane went to the D station with a Silleroid.

'Hello, I am Kelly. I'll be your combat partner. Let's begin.' Dane nodded. Then Dane fixed his sword to his belt, wore his boots and bracelet.

'Begin!' Ryan shouted. 'Okay, so let's start with the boots. There are two uses for the boots. One for transport and then dodge to attacks,' Kelly said. He was wearing the same things as Dane.

'Okay, but then what's the point of the bracelet?'

'Wait, don't jump to another weapon so quickly. Okay, so now I'll punch, and you run sideways. I'll keep punching, and you keep dodging,' Kelly said punching. Dane first fell to the ground with that punch. 'You need to concentrate, your highness!' Dane then dodged the punches after that quite well.

'Now, I'll teach you to use the band. All you need to do is concentrate, like this!' Kelly just closed his eyes to do that. He disappeared!

'Uh . . . Kelly, where are you? Ryan! Ryan! Ryan! Falsewagen and Woolaf are doing something! Kelly disappeared!'

Suddenly, something hit him hard. 'An invisible foe doesn't mean that there is no foe.'

'Kelly, you are alive!'

'Of course, I am!'

Kelly appeared again. 'Okay, now you try! Just focus . . . concentrate. Close your eyes.'

Hours passed, but Dane did not disappear, but then suddenly.

'Your highness, where did you go?'

'Yes! I did it! I disappeared!'

'Of course, you did. You need to touch the band to get back to visibility. Now, let's just go to the next weapon. Yes, the Absorn sword, just touch the tip to any material pressing the red gem . . . like this floor for instance.'

As Kelly touched the sword to the floor, it turned in to solid cobalt.

'Okay, here is your practicing bag,' Kelly said and gave him a dummy to practice on.

Kelly went out of the ring to observe him. Dane.

Dane pressed the gem, and the sword was made of cobalt too. 'Okay, I am pumped . . . hiyaaa!' The dummy didn't move a bit, instead, it started moving and got a normal sword in its hand.

'Huh?' Dane was very confused. Then the dummy attacked him! Dane ducked.

'Huh? Kelly, why is this nonliving thing attacking a living human being whose life is more precious than a rug?' Dane asked.

'Human, let me make a psychic note of that word. Oh, yes sir. It is a practicing bag. Of course it will attack! Don't uhhh . . . what was that word again? Yes! Don't you humors (meant to say humans) know that?' Kelly said feeling very very proud of him.

'Okay, this will be the final time in this chapter. Huh?'

***

STARVING YET FULL

'Oh my goodness! I'm starving! Let's go and eat' Trench said.

'Your wish is my command!' Ryan said clapping his hands.

'Wow! So much food!' Susan said with her mouth open.

'Our best royal cooks have made these. Please be seated! Oh, yes. First, you must try the Clobber fish. It is today's special!' Ryan said unrevealing a plate. It was a red colored fried yummy big . . . lizard?

'Ahhh! A lizard! A lizard! Kill it quick!' Susan yelled jumping out of her seat and running all around the place.

'My princess, please settle down. I do not know why you are calling this wonderful fish a 'lizard' whatever that is, but it is already dead. You can't kill—' Susan actually went over him and continued running.

'Susan, chill. Look, look I'm covering it,' Dane said covering it.

'Hmmmm . . . tasty! Tastes just like chicken.' Trench said as Susan and Dane looked at him, disgusted.

'Is everything like this?'

'Oh, no, your majesty. In fact, everything is better! We have smoked cockroach, cocoon salad, and for desert, cool rat juice!'

'I think I just lost my appetite!' Susan said.

'Give everything to Trench. I think we will pass,' Dane said.

Ryan nodded and started serving Trench.

'Idea!' Dane suddenly yelled. 'Ryan, can you teleport the bag I bought here?'

'Of course, I can!' Ryan said snapping his fingers and whoosh! The big yellow colored Duffle bag was . . . wait . . . on Dane!

'Ahhh! Help me! I think I am going to break my spine! What are you looking at? Help me!'Dane yelled as if he saw batman doing classical dance.

Susan helped him up, and Ryan apologized.

'Why do you want it anyway?' Susan asked.

Dane knelt down and opened the bag. 'Wait for it . . . wait for it . . . ta-da!' He took out ten packets of chips, microwavable popcorn, five boxes of salads, and a lot of more stuff that if I write, I would fill up this book and also the upcoming sequels! Susan's mouth remained wide open.

'That is a lot of food!' Trench said who was now standing beside Ryan.

'Nope, only a quarter of what I actually have.' Dane said opening a family pack of lemon-flavored chips. 'Dig in!'

First, Dane took a plateful of chips.

Then Susan took a handful.

And just when Trench's hand went in the packet, Susan shouted, 'Trench, no! You've eaten six clobber fish, a dozen smoked cockroaches, and twelve entire plates of that cocoon salad!'

'Eighteen plates of cocoon salad actually princess!'

'Yeah, whatever! If you eat even a little bit more, you'll die.'

'It's okay, Susan. Let him eat. You want to die anyway!'

'Yeah! But we want to die together!'

'Okay, but remember you cannot die here by an illness!'

'Okay, okay, I give up. Eat all you want Trench!

'Thanks!' Trench said taking so much from the packet that only two were left for Dane.

Dane shrugged and greedily gobbled both of the chips in the speed of light.

***

SPELLS!

Four days had passed since the first day of their practice. Trench ate all the delicacies of Vidhuslovia while Susan and Dane ate the food in Dane's duffle bag.

Each one of them had mastered their own weapons perfectly, and each of them also had learnt one spell.

Susan had learnt 'Tornado' in which she created a tornado and shot it at the opponent or could also control the tornado to do whatever she wanted it to do.

Trench had learnt 'Gravity', a spell in which he could control gravity and lift his opponent (not himself or not many people at a time).

Dane had learnt . . . err . . . well, he was learning a spell, 'Elementrick', which was the strongest spell that ever existed in Silleroid history. Even Ryan didn't know about it.

***

THE ATTACK ON VIDHUSLOVIA

'Your highness, you can do it you just need to concentrate, concentrate.'

Dane heard Kenny's hazy voice as he had closed his eyes. He then finally opened his eyes; he was sweating.

Suddenly, a big voice roared.

'Was that Mrs. Witched or what?' Susan yelled.

'Oh goodness of Norm! They are here!' Ryan yelled.

'Who is here?' Trench asked.

'Woolaf and Falsewagen,' Dane said.

'I'm going to make a psychic announcement and ready the armies. Kelly, you hide the princes and princess.'

'Yes, Minister Ryan as you wish. Let's go your highnesses!' Kelly transported them near him. 'Everybody, hold my hands and make a chain.'

Everybody held Kelly's hand except Dane.

'No! I'm not letting this kingdom face doom without me. I shall come too, Ryan!' Dane yelled.

'Don't talk nonsense at this moment your highness. You shall be hidden! You, at least, need a month of training, and you've only trained for a week.'

'I don't care!' Dane had never looked so angry. 'This is my command—'

'Time to go!' Kelly said.

The next moment, when the trio blinked, they were in a luxurious small room made of stone. They were wearing normal human clothes. The room had only four windows on the four sides of room and that too were with iron bars.

'Uhhh damn!' Dane yelled and kicked the golden bed.

'What can we do about it now, Dane? What is the use of showing anger now?' Susan said sitting on a chair.

'Yeah, man just chill,' Trench said.

'Chill? Have you gone mad or what? We are on a room at the top of the castle tower, and my dad is alive, and I can actually save him!' Danes face had turned red; his eyes were burning with anger! Then he realized that he was shouting and cooled down. 'We need to get out of here. I don't know how, but we need to.'

'That's next to impossible, Dane,' Susan said.

'Yeah, we don't even have our weapons or other stuff,' Trench said.

Suddenly, Dane got an idea and said, 'But we do have our spells right? If we all agree to it, we can escape this place.'

'No, It's dangerous outside,' both of them said together.

'Guys, please, okay, you just help me break these iron rods and you can stay here?'

Dane pleaded.

After a lot of time, they nodded.

'Let's do this!'

***

BREAKOUT

'Okay, I know what to do now, Trench, cast your spell on the window and pull out the iron bars, then Susan, I can sit on your tornado and go down. Okay?'

'Okay!' Trench and Susan said as if it were some traditional army camp.

Trench braced himself and yelled, 'Gravity!'

And just as planned, the iron bars came off.

'Susan, your turn,' Dane said.

'Tornado!' Susan yelled and shot the tornado outside the window and signaled Dane to sit on it.

Dane's hair was flying. It seemed like a perfect scene from an action film.

'You sure I won't fall down from the tornado?' Dane asked.

Susan shrugged.

He slowly went on the tornado and sat on it.

'Okay, now drop me down,' Dane ordered.

Susan nodded.

And there he went.

***

FAILED BATTLE

Dane was now on ground, fifty miles below that room. He saw that the towers were burning or broken. He saw that the small huts were burnt. The cultivation had been completely destroyed.

His eyes were burning with anger.

He prepared his feet for a long run. Just as he got in his sprinting position, someone tapped on his shoulder. 'Leaving without us?'

Danes eyes widened and he turned back with his eyes closed and with a fist, 'Hiyaaa!'

It was actually Trench. 'Ow ow ow ow! It hurts a lot. I think I broke my nose! What's your problem man!'

'Oh! Sorry! I thought it was Woolaf or Falsewagen!'

Trench overcame his pain.

'He's fine,' Susan spoke for him.

'Why'd you come down?'

'We couldn't leave a friend to fight two huge siler—whatever, could we?' Trench said.

Dane nodded. 'Okay, first, we need to get to the arena and get our stuff, and then we go save this kingdom and also the army, okay?'

Trench and Susan agreed.

They finally reached the arena, and thankfully, they didn't see either Woolaf or Falsewagen on their way, but they constantly heard their roars.

They quickly wore their armor and accessories and belted their weapons then zoomed to the place where the two maniacs were causing trouble.

'Brother! Why are we wasting killing these ants? Let's drink the chemicals and get out of here!' The smaller one said.

Though they were ten times bigger than the other Silleroids, they both still differed in physical appearance.

The small one was short in height and was also intelligent with a pudgy, flat face and well . . . looked . . . err . . . cute. His skin was like that of a tiger with hint of blue. He was probably Woolaf.

The bigger one (who was probably Falsewagen) was fitter than Woolaf. And looked handsomer than him too, but he seemed to be dumb. He had a vicious beard, the skin that seemed of a lion but a little bluish.

'Yes, brother! We could get that solution!' Falsewagen said.

Woolaf slammed his face with the club he was holding. 'Not "could" and "should" brother, there is a difference. "Could" means that you can, but "should" means—'

'No! Stop! Me no liked the English grammar and stuff! Let's go drink the chemical and stuff!'

Then, they both walked a little, uttered some words, slammed into the ground, and fell into an underground chemical lab.

'Save the lab!' Ryan shouted who was on a flying large yellow cockroach.

The not so much left army ran towards the lab in full speed but couldn't reach on time.

Thunder rumbled, the sky became grey, and you could hear animals (whichever they were) going crazy.

'Buwahahaha! Now no one can stop us!'

Then from inside the lab came Falsewagen. No, wait, he was leopard skinned. He had black long, ponytailed hair, and had the ears of Woolaf, just like a pug. He was holding a golden scepter with a green ball. His mighty limbs were wrapped with muscle. And finally, he had the wings of Woolaf, bat-like but red. He was now twenty times bigger than before! (He still looked like the bad ogre from *Shrek*.)

'We are one now, one-fourth of Woolaf's brain and three-fourths of Falsewagen! And also the same with my . . . sorry, our appearance! Looking good, right? We shall be known as Falselaf now!'

'This is terrible, but I'm going to fight now!' Dane said running towards him.

'Hey, Falselaf! I want to battle you now!'

Falselaf

Even Trench and Susan came running behind him and did the same.

'Ohohohoho! We . . . I see you got new rulers! Well, I'll take them with me then!' Falselaf stepped towards them.

'Army! Protect the rulers! Now!' Ryan yelled from above.

The army seemed surprisingly fast now, and they covered them.

'Hahaha! You think this wall of ants can stop me?'

He just blew them off with a single puff!

Then he took them in his fist and pounded their heads to his chest.

The trio braced for the impact.

Boom!

Chest Cage?

Dane slowly managed to open his eyes. He was on a rocky surface and saw two blurred images sitting in front of him.

'Hey, Dane! Susan, he's awake!'

'Oh! Dane, wake up, wake up!'

Dane sat down upright.

'Guys, what is happening? Where are we?'

Dane asked now conscious.

'I have no idea! But Trench is just saying creepy stuff,' Susan said rolling her eyes.

'It is true. I think Falselaf's chest was actually an internal cage. So when he slammed us on his chest, we actually want through and fell in a cage inside his chest. I don't think he was trying to kill us, you remember? He said that he'll take us with him.'

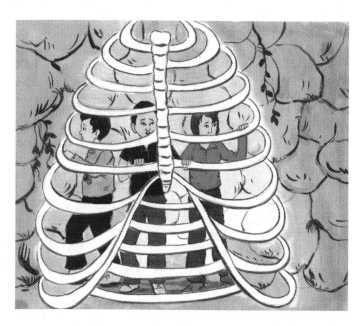

Trench said as if he was solving a case in which someone stole Queen Elizabeth's crown jewel.

Dane shrugged. 'Whatever, we need to find out whether we are with Falselaf. We need to find my father!'

'I wonder what Aunt Margaret would tell us to do now,' Trench says casually.

'Who Aunt Margaret?' Dane asked curiously.

'Who is Aunt Margaret? I don't know any Aunt Margaret! Though the name sounds funny Marga—' Susan was interrupted by Trench.

'Tell him Susan, no point hiding it now!'

'But . . . But . . . *sigh* Okay, Dane, Aunt Margaret was a secret agent, and she had adopted us and raised us. She taught us how to use weapons. I specialized in bow and arrow while Trench was good with a trident, so we had no doubt that what weapons we needed to take.'

Then Dane said, 'Ummm . . . Why did you need to hide that?'

Then Trench said, 'First reason, she is a secret agent. I don't think that we are supposed to tell that to anybody. But the main reason is that she was a traitor to USA. She worked with a terrorist organization. She was trying to use us as weapons against our own country. She was trying to use us as suicide bombers.'

Dane had blown his head off. He had been a friend to people who were raised up by a terrorist and had ultra experience in weapons. They were hardcore!

Then Susan continued, 'We, but one day, were playing hide and seek when Trench found this enormous secret room with many plans to destroy USA. Open fires, rockets, suicide bombers, then we found our name. We were furious, angry, mad at her and also . . . sad. We couldn't believe that an aunt who was so lovable had tried to kill us and also destroy our beloved nation. We then killed her.'

Nothing . . . silence, no one spoke.

Until Trench said, 'But after that there were many inspections at our house and we were found, with no guardian nor parents. We were sent to St. Jackson Orphanage. But then luck got worse; the older kids made us do all the work. They hit us with blades. It hurt a lot, and I used to cry at nights. Then we decided to run, and we came to your school. Your principal saw us, and I told him that we needed education. We needed to change what could happen in the future. I told him our story with different names of people and twisting the story a little . . . a lot. He took us as a special case.'

Two hours of silence, until—

'Come out, come out from my chest!' Falselaf's hand came through the front walls of the cage took all of them out.

Then, He dropped them in another cage. 'Hope you had a wonderful time in my chest. Now, you live here till I get one more.' He said going to a marvelously built castle.

'So we were in his chest!' Susan exclaimed.

'Told you!'

DAD

They all had been relieved from that story and were in a small cellar. Outside, they saw barren land for miles with no cultivation expect a type of weird plant that looked like cactus, but was silver; it stung their eyes.

Then they both looked at Dane; he was staring at something and remained speechless.

There was another human there sitting and eating from his plate.

Then, he looked up; he had a beard and was in casual human clothes with a lab coat.

'Oh, humans! Kids, you shouldn't have come down here. Did your fathers abandon you or something?'

'Uhhh . . . excuse me, if your son came down to find you, would you be proud of him?'

Susan asked.

'My son? No, I don't think so. But if he came down for me, I would be proud!' He answered.

Then Susan secretly hi-fived Trench.

'Da . . . dad? I'm Dane, your son,' Dane said with tears coming out of his eyes.

Norm Kenzy

Norm dropped his plate on the ground and ran towards Dane and hugged him tightly. 'Oh! Dane! You don't know how I've missed you and your mother all these years!'

After a lot of crying and emotional dialogues, Dane explained Norm everything.

'Oh, oh, Cantend is in a lot of danger. Woolaf and Falsewagen were dangerous alone, but now that they are together, no one can stop them,' Norm said thoughtfully.

'But, uncle, why doesn't he just kill us?' Trench asked.

'And he said that he needed one more. What one more? Ice cream? ☺' Susan asked.

'No, no, they are planning an experiment. They are collecting five human beings; they will take our brains, make it into a serum, and inject it into him. Then, they'll become super intelligent. We'll become his slaves. And by his intelligence, he will create 100000000000000000000000000 and a lot more of Silleroids and become the king of all of Cantend.'

'Ahhh . . . That's pretty intense. How do we stop him dad?' Dane asked.

'We can't do anything unless he finds the fifth human being. These iron bars are unbreakable. But we can practice our strengths and increase them.'

'But how? This is such a small room.' Trench asked.

Then, Norm clapped thrice, and the back walls of the jail opened.

There was a very big room with all sorts of equipment.

The trio's mouth remained open.

'What do you think I used to do when I got bored? I built this!'

'But what if they see this?' Susan asked.

'They won't. In fact, the only time I saw him before he brought you today was twenty-three years ago!'

'What about food?' Dane asked.

'Oh, they were kind enough to provide us with the Microfoody 2000 which I had made for them. You type on this Microfoody 2000 whatever you want, and it comes out of the small slit. In fact, I was eating bacon and eggs when you guys came in!'

'Okay, so this mission will be called mission "Save Cantend",' Dane said

'YES!' All of them shouted together.

***

Mission 'Save Cantend' Begins!

From the next day, they started serious training.

Susan was getting better and used to the ring and bow.

Trench was getting balanced on his hover board and was also attacking better with his trident now.

Dane was getting used to the attacking dummy. And also was getting used to the sword. He also used to trouble all of the other people by getting invisible. He also practiced Elementrick and the outcome?

NOTHING.

Even Norm was practicing something. He had made several formulae. Like for example, The sleepy potion that made the opponent really sleepy and drowsy.

Or the confusion potion with what he could confuse anybody. And so on . . .

'Guys! Time for dinner!' Norm called, and the trio came running from inside the gym and clapped thrice to close the secret gym door.

'I'll have spinach custard and carrot juice. And Trench will have the same.' Susan said typing on the Microfoody.

'But,' Trench tried to say, but Susan just showed him her hand.

'Okay, so I'll have a double layered cheese pizza.'

Dane started to say but was pushed aside by Norm, and he started typing.

'No, Dane, you'll have lima beans and broccoli juice. You need to remain fit. And I'll have three slices of cheese pizza,' Norm said.

'But you didn't allow me!' Dane whined.

'Yeah, but I've been having healthy food since twenty-three years you know. I'm taking it as an occasion today!' Norm replied handing Dane his plate and taking his.

Dane sighed eating a piece of the lima beans and made a disgusted face.

Trench and Susan giggled.

***

A Humu . . . M?

'Hiyaaa!' The trio yelled using their own personal weapons, when sounds were heard.

Thump! Thump! Thump!

'Impossible!' Norm dropped to a whisper. 'It's Falselaf! Get out! Quick! He has found another human.'

The trio sprinted out of the room, and Norm clapped thrice quickly.

Falselaf approached the caged room with an enormous, creepy, and mischievous smile.

'Hahahaha!' He said punching his chest, and a person dropped into his palm. 'This inferior female human was foolish enough to come down! I'll start my master plan tomorrow, and I shall rule!'

He pushed the human into the cage.

The trio and Norm's eyes were opened wide and their mouths too.

She was a blue eyed woman wearing a blue shirt and blue jeans and a blue striped cap. She looked at them with tears in her eyes. It was Elsa.

The trio and Norm hugged her tight.

'Oh, Elsa! I'm so happy to see you right now! But you shouldn't have come down here!' Norm wept.

'Yah mom, you shouldn't have come down here!' Dane said, and Trench and Susan repeated.

'I couldn't live without you people up there, and they treated me like a queen. Only for a week though! I got trained in martial arts and also in witchcraft since I didn't like their weapons!' Elsa said smiling.

After that, there was half an hour of silence.

***

FINAL DAY OF PRACTICE

Norm then declared, 'Okay, today, I name our team Penta! Today is our final day of training. Tomorrow, it's win or lose—your life day!'

'Training?' Elsa asked looking at the size of the room.

'Oooh, oooh, I'll show her!' Trench said and clapped his hands twice and behold . . . the training room!

The training had started. All of them went a little forward.

Norm had made many new potions.

Elsa learnt a whole lot of new spells.

Trench figured out many tricks with his trident.

Susan had learnt about angles of shooting.

Dane had learnt to manage his Absorn sword perfectly and also managed to cut the punching bag a little bit with Elementrick.

Now all of them were ready for the next day.

***

BREAKING OUT OF THE KETTLE

Thump! Thump! Thump!

The Penta woke up, startled.

'Buwahahaha!' Falselaf yelled. 'I have done it! I shall rule today!' He took the Penta out of the Cage and marched towards the large castle.

The castle was as filthy as a pig's house.

Then they reached an underground lab.

There was an enormous machine. It was a sort of silver kettle with wires and a helmet.

'You shall be separated from your brain, and the brains will become a serum and travel to my brain.' Falselaf laughed and pushed them into the kettle. He was excited so much that he forgot to take their weapons.

It was getting hot.

'Anyone has a plan?' Susan asked

'If we can somehow freeze this place, our weapons can make a small hole. And we can get out,' Dane said.

Reader, before we go forward, I shall give you a reminder of the Penta's weapons.

Norm- potions and gadgets

Elsa- witchcraft

Trench- a trident can create natural disasters which will only hit the target, a pair gloves which make a wall, and a foldable hover board. And a spell 'Gravity', in which he could control gravity and lift his opponent (not himself, or not many people at a time).

Susan- a bow shoots arrows that follow the one it was aimed at, a ring that creates a shield, which deflects attacks, and shoes with which she can jump really high. Her spell 'Tornado' in which she created a tornado and shoot it at the opponent or could also control the tornado to do whatever she wanted it to do.

Dane- Absorn sword, it absorbs any solid material its tip touches, the The Runon boots, wearing this, he could run at a speed of 950000 km per hour, and he could run on anything, and the Touchyinvis band, it madehim invisible and untouchable whenever he wanted. 'Elementrick' no one knows about it.

So, let's go on with the chapter.

'Hmmm . . . Let's see,' Norm said thoughtfully. 'Everybody try their spells and weapons on the wall, and let's see if it works out.'

The Penta agreed.

First, Elsa came forward. 'Let's see if I remember. They had taught me a freezing spell . . . Uhhh . . . Frusta!' A small cloud was created near the wall, and it snowed at that particular part of the wall.

'No, Elsa, we need more ice,' Norm said.

The cloud was then blown away.

Then Susan stretched and yelled. 'Tornado!' energy rushed from her hands, but nothing happened. And then she focused on the part of the wall and shot arrows. But the arrows bounced from the wall, and there was barely a scratch on the wall.

Then Dane came forward confidently, and yelled, 'Elementrick!' and of course you know what happened!

The wall blasted and they escaped to save Vidhuslovia.

No, that didn't happen, reader, the moment Dane yelled out his spell, nothing happened.

Dane, then depressed touched his Absorn sword to the wall, and it changed into pure whatever the kettle was made of.

Then he slashed the wall as hard as he could 'Hiyaaa!' but only a dent was made on the wall. 'How did the doofus manage to make this thing?' Dane asked frustrated and Norm shrugged. "Technically, I made it . . ."

Dane was surprised, "You work for him! Ahhhh!!!

Norm then said, "Son, you have to chill in life, he forced me . . ."

Trench says, "Makes Sense . . . Sort of . . ."

Dane walked back, signaling Trench to go forward.

Trench was going to say his spell when Norm said, 'No, Trench, if you lift the kettle, Falselaf will become aware of what we are doing in here.'

Trench nodded. It was getting really hot, if they didn't hurry; they would be brain syrup.

Trench focused his trident on a small part of the wall and thought of a blizzard. Then, his trident started to move a lot, and its pointed tops shot a beam that hit that part, and that part started freezing.

The Penta hi-fived each other.

'Now, we shall save Vidhuslovia!' Norm yelled.

'No, Norm, we should first wear our travelling gadgets, in case of a pursuit,' Elsa said.

The Penta agreed.

Norm pressed a button on his watch, and his lab coat became a jetpack.

Dane put on his Runon boots.

Trench unfolded his hover board.

Susan put on her weird shoes.

And then, everybody stared at Elsa. She didn't have anything to travel on.

But, then, she hit the floor with her right foot and yellow smoke puffed out . . . and lo! There was a broom in her hand.

'It flies, no worries,' Elsa said.

Then the trio got their weapons ready.

'On the count of three,' Dane said, '1 . . . 2 . . . 3!'

They attacked vigorously with their weapons and furious weird, white energy flashed, and within no time, there was a small hole on that part of the wall.

Pursuit!

The Penta sneaked out carefully without saying a word.

They looked at Falselaf. He was sleeping soundly. They also realized now that there was meter sort of thing on the kettle. It was a thermometer. It was on ninety-three degrees Celsius!

They had been in a kettle that was ninety-three degrees hot! Now, they thought that they could bear anything.

They quietly, but quickly, escaped the palace, and all of the other people started following Norm.

'Umm . . . Dad? Do you know where you are going?' Dane asked.

'Of course, I do!' Norm yelled. 'I know Cantend like the back of my hand!'

'Errr . . . Dad you have nothing on the back of your hand!' Dane said, while running he saw the scenery. There were volcanoes, a few lava bodies, frozen lakes, and also weird cactuses.

After ten minutes of travelling, Susan who was jumping randomly said, 'Did any of you hear that?'

'Nope, nothing,' all of the others said.

Then suddenly, *thump! Thump!*

The Penta was alarmed and stopped to look back.

A big fat figure with wings was running . . . no . . . flying . . . no . . . doing both and coming towards the Penta!

'Falselaf,' Norm and Dane said together.

'We'll fight!' Dane said enthusiastically.

'No, Dane, we are not strong enough. We need to reach Vidhuslovia and take the help of the army.' Norm said.

'But, uncle, most of the army was destroyed during our capture!' Trench said.

'Yeah… and the other half was destroyed when I was captured!' Elsa said apprehensively.

'No problem. I had put a chemical in their physical structure, which gave them super healing powers. Even if their whole skin was torn and their skeletons were crushed, they would be perfectly fine and ready to fight in a sharp eighteen hours and 8.7 minutes,' Norm said, promptly. 'For now, we need to flee. Look, he is gaining on us.'

Falselaf was now only twenty meters away from them (a.k.a. pretty close)!

They now boosted behind Norm like a bullet train that doesn't have breaks.

'You pesky little royal brats think you can fool Falselaf the great!' Falselaf roared, eventually increasing his speed, getting influenced by the running Penta.

'Nope, we, pesky little royal brats, think that we can fool Falselaf, the beast from 'Beauty and the Beast'!' Dane yelled at him.

The others giggled.

'Huh! I don't know what you talk about, but it makes the Falselaf angry!' Falselaf roared louder this time and was red in the face.

'No, Dane, don't make him angry. You wouldn't want him to be angry,' Norm said in a really serious tone.

'Okay, dad!' Dane said.

Falselaf was only five meters away from them now!

'I never thought I would do this. I don't think this will work . . . an untested teleporter. Here it goes!' Norm said nervously.

He took out a red small machine from his lab coats pocket. It looked like a Chinese puzzle box with a neon blue button.

Norm said nothing. He just sighed and pressed a button on the thing.

The Penta disappeared in a blink!

BACK TO THE ORIGIN

Norm was right, although, his teleporter did work, but it was untested. 'Yes!' Norm yelled. 'My teleport worked!'

'Mm . . . guys, I think we should start screaming,' Susan said. 'Why? Because my invention work—aaahhh!' Norm and the Penta started screaming when they saw down

They were falling to the deepest lava pond in Vidhuslovia!

'Ahhh!' Dane yelled. 'Ahhh!' Trench yelled. 'Ahhh!' Elsa yelled. 'Ahhh!' Susan yelled. 'Ahhh!' Norm yelled.

Till this time, they almost hit the lava when Whoosh!

Ryan, on the yellow cockroach, rushed like a meteorite promptly followed by an army just when Norm touched his feet to the floor.

'Your highnesses! You all are safe! I'm really happy!' Ryan said emotionally, and hugged Norm who was huffing and puffing like he was just on a goose chase.

Norm was right, (jinx!) the army was fully healed and was in perfect fighting condition without even a small bruise.

'Thank you for teleporting us to land Ryan, but don't be happy yet. Falselaf is coming here to Vidhuslovia, at top speed. By my calculations, he can be here in thirty minutes or less, if he gains speed. Or if we are lucky, he might just rest on his way here,' Norm said intensely.

'Yes, sire!' Ryan yelled.

'I shall lead the army,' Norm said.

'No, dad. We all shall lead the army. Vidhuslovia needs all of us!' Dane said.

Norm nodded with a wide grin on his face.

***

PLOTTING

The Penta, Ryan, the army, and also the trainers who had trained the trio were present in a large tent sort of thing.

'Okay, so Elsa and I shall defend the north of Vidhuslovia with a small part of the army. Trench will be at the east gate, Susan at the western gates, and Dane, you will be at the south gate. Is that clear?' Norm yelled.

'Yes, sir!' All the people . . . errr . . . living beings in the tent yelled.

It sounded like ten billion tanks were shooting at once.

'Wherever Falselaf enters from, Ryan will teleport every single person to that particular point at once!' Norm commanded and looked at Ryan, and he nodded.

'Now, run to your gates now!' Norm yelled. 'We have a kingdom to save!'

***

A KINGDOM TO SAVE!

Everybody was at their gates, some scared, some exited, and some thinking that 'Vidhuslovia is gone for sure.'

Dane was at his gate scared, sweating, and, most of all, angry.

He was damn angry on Falsewagen. He had kidnapped his dad, kept him hostage for twenty-three years, then kidnapped Dane himself and also his friends, and then took his mom.

Then kept them all in a kettle expecting to fry them up and inject their brains into himself.

And now, he was going to destroy his permanent home (as he knew he is not going back anyway).

'I am really really really **hungry!**'

Dane yelled.

'Your highness, I thought the author was saying that you're angry,' one of the army

men said.

'I am, but more than that, I am hungry!' Dane yelled.

'Sire, I have cake, if you want it. Your mother gave a piece to me,' the army man said handing over the piece of cake.

'Thank you very much, oh, kind fighter. I humbly accept this piece of cak—' He was interrupted by large   BOOM!

Falselaf blasted out of the gate. The piece of cake fell.

Dane quickly touched his sword to the ground, and it turned into solid gold. 'HEY! FALSELAF! WHAT IS YOUR PROBLEM MAN! YOU FIRST, KIDNAP MY DAD, THEN ME AND MY FRIENDS, THEN MY MOM, THEN YOU ATTACK MY HOME, AND NOW YOU DROP MY CAKE? I WILL NOT FORGIVE YOU FOR THIS!' The moment Dane finished his sentence, everybody was transported there.

'Wow! He is angry, man. He is angry,' Trench said.

'No, he is a hungry man!' Susan said with a smile.

'Attaaaaaaaack!' Norm yelled to his part of the army, and he started flying in the air. Elsa also started flying on her broom, and the army also charged at Falselaf.

Then Trench, Susan, and Dane also ordered their army to attack.

'Ha! You beings think you can beat me!' Falselaf yelled smacking his scepter on the army.

They came running back.

'We need to attack one by one!' Norm yelled. 'First, I shall go with Elsa and my part of the army, then Trench, followed by Susan, and then finally Dane! GO!'

First, Norm threw a poisoning potion at Falselaf, and that hardly tickled him!

'Is that all you got?' Falselaf yelled.

Then, Elsa yelled, 'Flamicane!' And a large hurricane of fire was blasted at Falsewagen!

Silence . . . was he defeated? Could this big monster die so easily?

As the fog cleared, a giant figure appeared again. It was Falsewagen. He would not fall so easily.

He stepped forward brushing his shoulder with his hand.

'You think that'll hurt me?' Falselaf roared taking Elsa in his palm.

'Mom!' Dane yelled, and he quickly became invisible with the help of his ring.

'Where did he go now—ow ow ow ow ow ow!' Falselaf bellowed in pain. His eye was bleeding, and he left Elsa.

Dane had poked him in his right eye with his solid gold sword and then reappeared.

'You still won't be able to defeat me! Thirty seconds and I will be back to normal! And you have your father to thank for that!' Falselaf said as he regained some health every second.

'These thirty seconds should not go to waste! Guys! Attack with whatever you've all got!' Norm yelled!

Every single person attacked Falselaf vigorously. They pierced his body, shot arrows, froze him, burnt him, and also dropped him from a very long height in those small thirty seconds.

Falselaf didn't even move—not a bit. No one was saying anything. Falselaf wasn't even breathing.

I don't think anyone was breathing. Falselaf was dead; the battle was won!

Or was it?

THE BLACK TRUTH

The black truth is, all of this was a lie, nothing of this happened, did it?

Nah! Just playing with you guys!

So, let's continue with the story.

Just when everybody was going to go bonkers partying, a green emerald necklace appeared around Falsewagen. He was transforming into something different.

'Oh, no, no, no, no, no . . . this cannot be happening!' Norm was nervous.

'What's up, dad?' Dane asked coolly.

'You see the emerald necklace on his neck?'

'Yes, wasn't it always there?' Dane asked innocently.

'You haven't been paying attention, Dane!' Norm yelled as Falselaf kept changing. 'No, it hasn't always been there. I had given both, Falsewagen and Woolaf this necklace, It held their internal power. I had locked millions of lives and spirits. Whenever they needed help, the necklaces gave them ultimate power and made them almost invincible. I thought that they had thrown it when I—'

'CHEATED US! WE ALWAYS KNEW ABOUT THESE NECKLACES NORM! WE ONLY DIDN'T KNOW WHAT IT DID! BUT WE THOUGHT ABOUT IT AND REMEMBERED THAT YOU SAID THAT THERE WAS A REPLICA OF THE EMERALD SAFE INSIDE A DIAMOND BOX HIDDEN SOMEWHERE AND YOU SAID IT IS FOR THE SAFETY OF VIDHUSLOVIA, SO WE KNEW THAT IT IS POWERFUL! WE FOUND SOME INVISIBILITY SPRAY IN YOUR LAB AND MADE IT INTO TWO CLUBS, THEN MY SCEPTRE, AND NOW, IT'S TRUE FORM—THE NECKLACE!' It was Falselaf, and he did not look like the absurdly funny but giant dwarf from Cinderella like before now. But now, he was damn scary. You could melt if you just saw his snarl.

He was black in colour, as sleek as paper. He was shaped like a shadow only ten thousand times bigger. He had really creepy, fiery red eyes. His teeth were incredibly white; he could make a man blind just by smiling. The bat wings of his were perfectly in shape, and he was flying smoothly. His speed was impeccable!

The Penta was thrilled by his look!

'Now it may be almost impossible to defeat you Falselaf, but you gave yourself away. I didn't even remember about that emerald till today!' Norm said with a half grin and half crybaby face.

Falselaf face palmed himself.

'Yes, and now, Dane!' Norm said,

'Huh? What! Who killed whom? Peanut butter jelly, sugar, and tomato sauce! Pancakes!'

'Dane, snap out of it!' Dane was so scared because of that monsters appearance that he had gone bonkers! 'Yeah, dad?' Dane finally asked.

'I will send you telepathic instructions to you, and you follow them to the emerald it will—Aaarrgghhh!' Norm was hurled up by Falselaf and was now in his fist and was being squeezed.

'Oh, no you won't!' Falselaf yelled.

'Dad!' Dane climbed his feet and up to his face.

He slashed him loads of times!

'Ha! You almost tickled me!' Falselaf said and tossed him up like a ball and hit him with his scepter like he was playing baseball!

***

EMERALD RETRIEVAL

Dane fell where he thought China was up there. He tried to get up, but it was very difficult to. He had taken the impact directly on his left leg.

He tried to get up and finally did but fell again in no time. He had broken his calf. His pants were eerily red because of blood.

'Dane, I know you can hear me! And I also know you are hurt! Ryan and all the other are keeping Falselaf busy. You need to reach the back entrance main castle first'. As soon as Dane heard this, he knew it was Norm trying to give him instructions to get to that emerald.

Now, he tried to get up again with his sword as a support; he limped to the well first and poured some water on his thigh.

He continued his limping journey to the main castle, just when an enormous boulder landed right in front of him. He looked at the direction from which it was hurled at him.

It was Falselaf; Trench had created a wall with the help of his gloves. Falselaf didn't understand what was happening.

To distract him, Susan was making him fly on the tornado really high up and then released him. When he hit the ground, there was an enormous hole. Now he was LIVID!

'Argh!' He yelled as his eye became redder, and suddenly, he shot out fire from his eyes right at Susan!

'No!' Trench yelled with Dane.

As the smoke cleared, Susan was safe!

Ryan had teleported her behind Falselaf!

As Falselaf turned around, Trench made a volcano erupt right above his head!

'Argh!' He cried in pain.

'Dane, we have bought his attention. Go in the castle now!' Dane heard Norm's voice, and he entered the castle.

'Now, Dane, go to the grandfather's clock.'

Dane looked around and then limped up to the grandfather's clock, which was dead, but the pendulum was still strangely swinging.

'Pull the pendulum out Dane but softly.'

Dane did as he was told to, and behind the pendulum, there was a box with a weird symbol on it.

Dane wondered whether he should open it.

'Open it,' Norm said as if he read Dane's mind. *'You will find the emerald inside it, wear it.'*

Dane found an emerald inside it and following his father's instructions. He put the emerald on his Touchyinvis Band as it transformed into a golden chained bracelet with the emerald fitted right in the middle.

'Cool huh? Now come to the battle spo—'

'Dad!' Dane yelled.

The emerald glowed as his broken bone got healed, but there was no time to question how this happened.

He ran as fast as no one in the world and busted through Trench's wall.

Falselaf was going to smash Norm to the floor!

Dane jumped with all his might, and he punched Falselaf hard on the face. Blood spilled from his mouth as he fell down!

'Hehe . . . Now I have got a worthy opponent!' He said wiping the blood dripping off his chin.

'Norm, is this because of the emerald?' Elsa asked.

'No, it was because of the love for me and the anger on this monster the emerald's power would be not this strong. This was the power of love amongst us—more powerful than anything,' Norm said.

Falselaf shot out fire out of his eyes.

Dane was burning, but nothing protected him. He was being roasted.

'Dane!' Trench stepped forward to help him but stopped by Norm.

'Let him handle this,' he said.

Dane fell to his knees.

'That was pretty easy.' Falselaf smirked.

Suddenly, Dane mumbled something.

'What? No one can hear you,' Falselaf said.

'Elementrick!' Dane yelled, but nothing happened.

'No! Why has this happened? The attack should have been fully powerful!' Norm yelled. 'Attack everybody!' The army attacked.

As everybody yelled, Elsa, Norm, Trench, and Susan ran to Dane. He was bruised all over.

'Da . . . da . . . d . . . dad?' Dane said.

'Yes, Dane?' Norm said anxiously.

'I am really sorry. It is all my fault. I shouldn't have come to Cantend at first place.'

'No, Dane. It is not your fault. Don't blame yourself,' Norm said with tears. 'It was actually mine, if I never came to explore this place and created this race, nothing would happen.'

'No, da—'

Boom!

***

Memory Power

Falselaf had picked up all of them and squeezed them hard along with Ryan. Dane saw them shrieking in pain, helplessly. He couldn't do anything.

Dane thought, and then he yelled. 'Hey, Falselaf! Why are you acting like a coward? If you want to fight, fight with me! You won't get anything killing them! I know the secrets of our world, which makes us so intelligent!' Dane had no idea what was the 'secret'.

Falselaf stared at him with dull eyes. Then threw them down and picked up Dane furiously.

'Tell me the secrets, or I'll crush you to death!' Falselaf yelled shaking Dane back and forth.

'Try to kill me! If you kill me, the secrets will die with me!'

'You are right. I cannot kill you,' Falselaf said, slowly keeping him down. 'But I can kill your parents and friends!' Falselaf yelled quickly grabbing Ryan, Elsa, Norm, Trench, and Susan and squeezing them.

'Aaaaarrrggghhhh!'

They all yelled.

Their yells hurt Dane's ears. It was a frightening shriek.

'Tell me, boy!' Falselaf yelled. 'Or I will crush them!'

'No! I will tell you Falselaf. Just leave them.'

'No, I will not leave them. I know you are trying to fool me. You talk first, then I will leave them.' Falselaf shrugged.

'No, Falselaf. I am not dishonest like you. I will not do anything foolish. I know your power. You can turn me to dust in no time.' Dane said.

'Well, true story . . . you can't hurt me, but I shall not take any risk. I give you thirty seconds. Spill the beans!' Falselaf roared.

Dane thought hard; he didn't have any idea that what the 'secret' actually was. It just came out. Why did he do that; why couldn't he just have saved himself?

The green emerald started shining.

'Over! Now they die!' Falselaf yelled starting to throw them to the ground with real force.

If they even touched the ground, they would be smashed into a million pieces. Falselaf now was that high.

As they fell, the memories he spent with them came and went from his mind in a flash.

The emotional moments spent with Elsa and Norm.

The joyous time spent with Trench and Susan.

He remembered how they were together through sad times and good ones, through the scariest moments, and through the tensed ones. They were always with each other, risking lives, helping each other.

Now, he could not let them down.

As these memories went past, he ran so fast that he was invisible to the naked eye. He lift them all and put them safely at one corner.

He was glowing green. He had anger in his eyes.

'Falselaf! You wanted to know the answer. I will tell you!'

Falselaf looked anxiously towards Dane.

Dane jumped high until Falselaf's face. 'It is the love we share!' Dane yelled punching him tightly on his face as blood came out of Falselaf's mouth, and his head turned. He punched him again. 'It is because we care about each other!' Blood came out of Falselaf's mouth, and his head turned the other side. Dane took out his sword and slashed him furiously once, and Falselaf was knocked down!

Dane then dropped down on his legs.

Then, Falselaf got up weakly and started clapping slowly. He had a really big and deep cut on his cheek. The blood was dripping from his chin.

'Well done, Kenzy. The emerald has really made you strong. Now, I cannot defeat you. Although your army has fallen, you are still strong. I cannot defeat you, but I will kill your friends for sure!' He yelled clutching Ryan, Norm, Elsa, Susan, and Trench and squeezing them hard.

'No!' Dane yelled. 'You don't fail me now luck! ELEMENTRICK!'

You might have guessed what happened. Nothing, but, no. That did not happen. For the first time, 'Elementrick' worked.

Yes, go on, say 'What?', but it worked. Everyone in the fist of Falselaf teleported behind Dane.

As Dane dragged his right foot forward and stomped it on the ground, Falselaf flew up. 'What is this Black Magic?' Falselaf roared.

Dane put his hands open beside him, and his hands had green energy flowing, and his eyes were green. 'Black magic? More like power of love and care!' Dane then shot all of his energy like a beam!

Falselaf was thrown back with by the energy. Then he was thrown down. Before he hit the ground, he started to disappear!

'Aggghhh! Nooo! I cannot die I am invinci . . . ble,' he said. Dane ran with his super speed and slashed Falselaf's emerald with all his power.

Black and white rays of light came out of the emerald and formed different groups species.

Some looked like guinea pigs, while some looked like cupids, and there were many more. They ran off on seeing the atmosphere of the place.

The battle had been over. The villain had lost. Good had won, defeating the bad and evil. The story was complete with only a few chapters left.

***

CANTEND: SAVED

Dane, with a smile went to his friends. He was bleeding, yet happy.

'You have saved Vidhuslovia, Dane!' Norm and Elsa said in a chorus.

'You are the hero of the day, man!' Trench said, patting him on the back.

'Good job, Dane.' Susan yelled.

'Thanks, guys. I love you al, but can I go to the doctor Silleroid? I have a few broken bones.'

'Prince, you not only defeated Falselaf, but also mastered Elementrick!' Ryan said, 'Even though I think it was a one-time thing. Now, to the doctor!' And they all teleported to the doctor Silleroid.

Not So Much of A Happy Ending

Dane came out of the doctor's room, wearing bandage on his head and arms. He found Ryan, Susan, Trench, Elsa, and Norm sitting around a round table. The table had many pictures and pages of info.

'Sup, guys!' Dane said enthusiastically. 'Why so many long faces? Cantend is now safe from evil, right?'

'No, it isn't. We researched, and here is what we found.' Norm said showing Dane some pictures and papers. 'There were various lights coming out of Falselaf 's emerald, right?' Dane nodded.

'We realized that they all were spirits, good and bad. They were created into a sets of new forms of species. These are some pictures the CCTV cameras caught,' Elsa said showing him pictures.

'The Cupids. Innocent looking but evil and smart. They are the bad part of Falselaf, not entirely evil, but yeah. They are disaster makers. Their arrows can make two people hate each other, and if they want, they can send a person into an imaginary world of peril,' Susan said.

'The Guineas. Cute and dumb. They are normal earth guinea pigs, but they can talk. They mainly focus on farming and storing and do not like violence. They are the innocent and good spirits,' Trench said.

'The Treeks. They are regular trees that can talk. They stay in one place, meditating, and are very calm and composed. They don't use their powers, but if they get angry, they will unleash their psychic power,' Elsa said.

'Finally, the *Tromeros*—it is the Greek for terrible. These are the most evil species of all, with powers such as flight, super speed, super strength, psychic powers, and they can control the three main elements fire, water, and grass. But they don't attack without a plan. Or without a reason.' Norm ended.

'So we are safe, right? They have no reason to attack anyways.' Dane said with sweat on his forehead.

'Yeah!' Norm said a little relived.

'But now, Cantend will have not only Silleroids but many more species. More kingdoms will be made. Wars will happen, and Cantend will not be so empty and boring!' Ryan exclaimed.

'Main thing, we are safe, Falselaf has died. This calls for a—' Trench interrupted Norm.

'Celebration! Woohoo!'

'Yaaaaaay!' Susan and Dane yelled.

'I guess!' Ryan said.

***

FINALLY, THE END

The Penta was now at the royal dining hall of the main castle. Plates with food were flying all across the room, and the room was bustling with happiness. Silleroids were enjoying to there fullest!

'Let's take a seat!' Norm said as they got seated.

'Dane, I think the food is good!' Elsa said.

'Yeah, right!' Dane said sarcastically.

Then a few plates flew to them. They were filled with rice, salads, pizzas, and burgers—all human food!

'How is this—' Dane was interrupted by Susan. 'Possible!'

'Nah, the Silleroidian food was fine though!' Trench yelled.

'Well, you know, when I came to Vidhuslovia, I did not like their food either. So I taught them

how to cook human food, which they liked a lot!'
Elsa said, blushing.

Dane then yelled. 'Best day ever!'

***

THE END?

In Cantend, somewhere not known . . .

'Sire, the spies have returned. The Silleroids are not suspicious.'

'Stupendous! Silleroids, more like Sillyroids! We shall attack after the preparations are all in place. You will be crushed under me Kenzy, and revenge shall be mine!'

End